Bots

20,000 ROBOTS UNDER THE SEA

by Russ Bolts
illustrated by Jay Cooper

LITTLE SIMON

New York London Toronto Sydney New Delhi

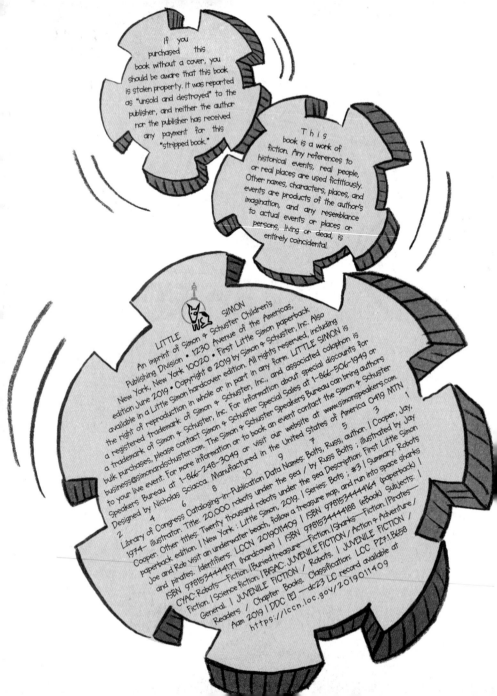

LITTLE SIMON
An imprint of Simon & Schuster Children's Publishing Division • 1230 Avenue of the Americas, New York, New York 10020 • First Little Simon paperback edition June 2019 • Copyright © 2019 by Simon & Schuster, Inc. Also available in a Little Simon hardcover edition. All rights reserved, including the right of reproduction in whole or in part in any form. LITTLE SIMON is a registered trademark of Simon & Schuster, Inc., and associated colophon is a trademark of Simon & Schuster, Inc. For information about special discounts for bulk purchases, please contact Simon & Schuster Special Sales at 1-866-506-1949 or business@simonandschuster.com. The Simon & Schuster Speakers Bureau can bring authors to your live event. For more information or to book an event contact the Simon & Schuster Speakers Bureau at 1-866-248-3049 or visit our website at www.simonspeakers.com. Designed by Nicholas Sciacca. Manufactured in the United States of America 0419 MTN

2   4   6   8   10   9   7   5   3   1

Library of Congress Cataloging-in-Publication Data Names: Bolts, Russ, author. | Cooper, Jay, 1974– illustrator. Title: 20,000 robots under the sea / by Russ Bolts ; illustrated by Jay Cooper. Other titles: Twenty thousand robots under the sea Description: First Little Simon paperback edition. | New York : Little Simon, 2019. | Series: Bots ; #3 | Summary: Robots Joe and Rob visit an underwater beach, follow a treasure map, and run into space sharks and pirates. Identifiers: LCCN 2019011409 | ISBN 9781534444171 (hardcover) | ISBN 9781534444164 (paperback) | ISBN 9781534444188 (eBook) Subjects: | CYAC: Robots—Fiction. | Buried treasure—Fiction. | Sharks—Fiction. | Pirates—Fiction. | Science fiction. | JUVENILE FICTION / Robots. | JUVENILE FICTION / Action & Adventure / General. | JUVENILE FICTION / Readers / Chapter Books. Classification: LCC PZ7.1.B658 Aam 2019 | DDC [E] —dc23 LC record available at https://lccn.loc.gov/2019011409

CONTENTS

But for me, right now, today is what we call a scorcher. That means it's the perfect time to go to the beach.

WELCOME TO THE BEACH

It's the same way on Mecha Base One, where our friends the Bots live.

"Who are the Bots?" you might ask. Well, that's a short story.

Many years ago, scientists on Earth created a space camera to see what was at the end of the universe.

They blasted the space cameras out into space and soon the rockets reached the end of the universe . . .

. . . where they found a planet!

The planet was called Mecha Base One and it was full of robots.

Two of these robots, or Bots as they like to be called, found the space cameras.

Hmm, they usually have more to say than that.

Oh no! It looks like they are leaking!

Wait, false alarm. They are not leaking. They are sweating because it is a scorcher on their planet today.

Humans think that Bots can stand the heat, but that is not true.

You see, it gets very hot on Mecha Base One.

One time it was so hot, one of Joe and Rob's teachers melted.

He was teaching the class how to build a star, but he mixed the wrong gases together.

The small star made the teacher go all ooey-gooey.

But that did not stop him from handing out homework!

Nothing stops teachers from handing out homework . . . even on alien planets.

Don't worry. The teacher was put back together, good as new. Well, almost good as new.

But back to our poor, roasting Bots.

There are ways to beat the heat, even on alien planets like Mecha Base One.

Make a robot icicle?

No.

Turn off the sun?

Please don't.

CLICK

Really strong fans?

Nope.

WHOOSH

No, there's only one way to beat a scorcher.
You've got to go to the beach.

CHAPTER 2

Beach Day

On Earth, the beach means this:

But on Mecha Base One, the beach is a little different. As far as we know, there is still sand and water, but where are all the Bots?

Let's follow Joe and Rob to find out.

Hmm, maybe the heat has fried the Bots' brains? This does not look crowded at all. It is totally empty.

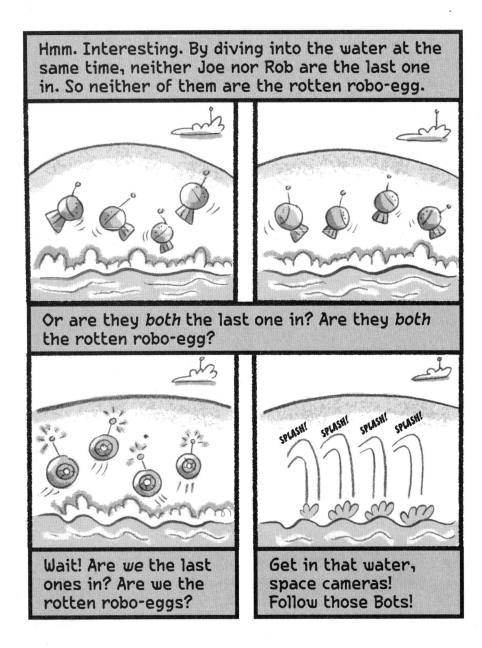

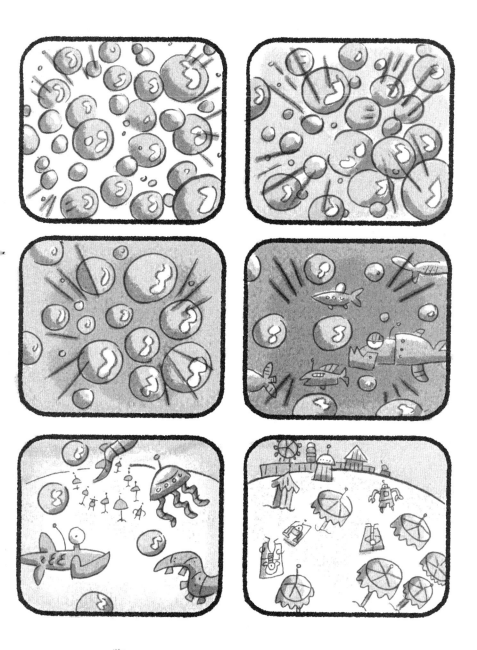

CHAPTER 3

Under the Sea

Well, I'll be! It's a robo-beach under the sea!

There are Bots playing Floppy-Diskee . . .

Bots playing Bot-chi and Volley-Botball . . .

Bots fishing . . .

Bots surfing . . .

There are even Bots building a sandcastle!

Wow, this water feels great!
It sure does! Nice and cool and . . . wait a minute . . .

Did the water just get a little warmer?
Umm, no, uh-uh, no way. Let's swim over there.

CHAPTER 4
X Marks the Spot

Joe and Rob were on an "already-buried" buried treasure hunt.

But their search was leading them into dark waters.

34

36

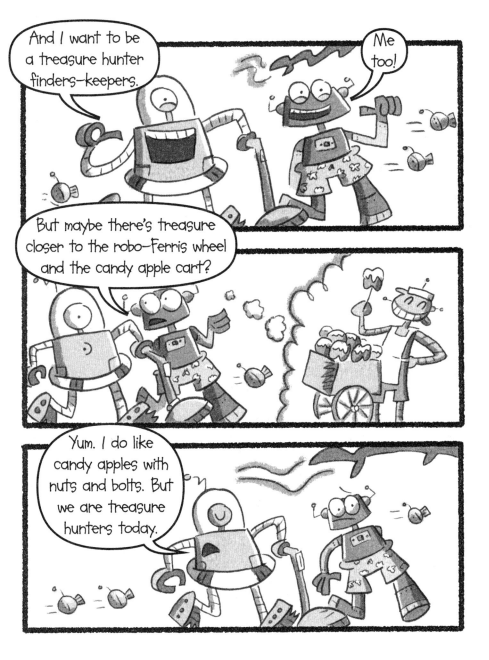

40

And so our two Bot heroes swam farther out into the sea searching for treasure. But they were not alone.

CHAPTER 5

I Scream Tinny

Treasure?! Those two Bots are going to find treasure without me? Not on my watch.

But Tinny Bot wasn't alone.

47

Earthlings, we know that our oceans are filled with all kinds of wild things.

Mecha Base One has all kinds of wild things in their ocean, too.

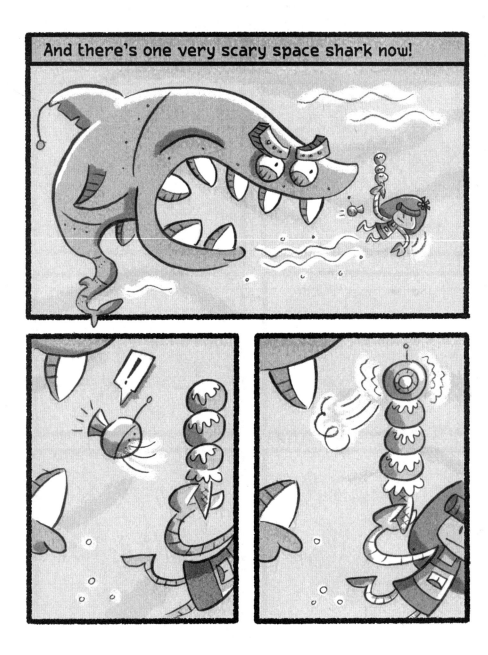

Aha! You see, I told you we were not the rotten robo-eggs!

60

CHAPTER 7

Blackboard the Pi-Robot

Remember when I said that things couldn't get worse for the Bots? I was wrong.

Blackboard is one of the scariest Pi-robots in all of Mecha Base One.

He has stolen ships. . . .

PLUCK!

NEIL WUZ HERE

Stolen flags . . .

Stolen treasure . . .

One time he even stole an entire jail!

That's where he got all his Pi-robot crew.

How do I know this? Easy.
Rob did a report on Pi-robots once.

76

79

80

91

103

Maybe we can find out more from Tinny?